INDUSTRIAL REVOLUTION

INDUSTRIAL REVOLUTION

by Poul Anderson

Ever think how deadly a thing it is if a machine has amnesia—or how easily it can be arranged . . . .

Hell, yes," Amspaugh admitted, "it was a unique war in many ways, including its origin. However, there are so many analogies to other colonial revolutions—" His words trailed off as usual.

"I know. Earth's mercantile policies and so forth," said Lindgren. He fancies himself a student of interplanetary history. This has led to quite a few arguments since Amspaugh, who teaches in that field, joined the Club. Mostly they're good. I went to the bar and got myself another drink, listening as the mine owner's big voice went on:

"But what began it? When did the asterites first start realizing they weren't pseudopods of a dozen Terrestrial nations, but a single nation in their own right? There's the root of the revolution. And it can be pinned down, too."

"'Ware metaphor!" cried someone at my elbow. I turned and saw Missy Blades. She'd come quietly into the lounge and started mixing a gin and bitters.

The view window framed her white head in Orion as she moved toward the little cluster of seated men. She took a fat cigar from her pocket, struck it on her shoe sole, and added her special contribution to the blue cloud in the room after she sat down.

"Excuse me," she said. "I couldn't help that. Please go on." Which I hope relieves you of any fear that she's an Unforgettable Character. Oh, yes, she's old as Satan now; her toil and guts and conniving make up half the biography of the Sword; she manned a gun turret at Ceres, and was mate of the *Tyrfing* on some of the earliest Saturn runs when men took their

5

lives between their teeth because they needed both hands free; her sons and grandsons fill the Belt with their brawling ventures; she can drink any ordinary man to the deck; she's one of the three women ever admitted to the Club. But she's also one of the few genuine ladies I've known in my life.

"Uh, well," Lindgren grinned at her. "I was saying, Missy, the germ of the revolution was when the Stations armed themselves. You see, that meant more than police powers. It implied a degree of sovereignty. Over the years, the implication grew."

"Correct." Orloff nodded his bald head. "I remember how the Governing Commission squalled when the Station managers first demanded the right. They foresaw trouble. But if the Stations belonging to one country put in space weapons, what else could the others do?"

"They should have stuck together and all been firm about refusing to allow it," Amspaugh said. "From the standpoint of their own best interests, I mean."

"They tried to," Orloff replied. "I hate to think how many communications we sent home from our own office, and the others must have done the same. But Earth was a long way off. The Station bosses were close. Inverse square law of political pressure."

"I grant you, arming each new little settlement proved important," Amspaugh said. "But really, it expressed nothing more than the first inchoate stirrings of asteroid nationalism. And the origins of that are much more subtle and complex. For instance . . . er . . . . "

"You've got to have a key event somewhere," Lindgren insisted. "I say that this was it."

A silence fell, as will happen in conversation. I came back from the bar and settled myself beside Missy. She looked for a while into her drink, and then out to the stars. The slow spin of our rock had now brought the Dippers into view. Her faded eyes sought the Pole Star—but it's Earth's, not our own any more—and I wondered what memories they were sharing. She shook herself the least bit and said:

"I don't know about the sociological ins and outs. All I know is, a lot of things happened, and there wasn't any pattern to them at the time. We just slogged through as best we were able, which wasn't really very good. But I can identify one of those wriggling roots for you, Sigurd. I was there when the question of arming the Stations first came up. Or, rather, when the incident occurred that led directly to the question being raised."

Our whole attention went to her. She didn't dwell on the past as often as we would have liked.

A slow, private smile crossed her lips. She looked beyond us again. "As a matter of fact," she murmured, "I got my husband out of it." Then quickly, as if to keep from remembering too much:

"Do you care to hear the story? It was when the Sword was just getting started. They'd established themselves on SSC 45—oh, never mind the catalogue number. Sword Enterprises, because Mike Blades' name suggested it—what kind of name could you get out of Jimmy Chung, even if he was the senior partner? It'd sound too much like a collision with a meteorite—so naturally the asteroid also came to be called the Sword. They began on the borrowed shoestring that was usual in those days. Of course, in the Belt a shoestring has to be mighty long, and finances got stretched to the limit. The older

7

men here will know how much had to be done by hand, in mortal danger, because machines were too expensive. But in spite of everything, they succeeded. The Station was functional and they were ready to start business when—"

*

It was no coincidence that the Jupiter craft were arriving steadily when the battleship came. Construction had been scheduled with this in mind, that the Sword should be approaching conjunction with the king planet, making direct shuttle service feasible, just as the chemical plant went into service. We need not consider how much struggle and heartbreak had gone into meeting that schedule. As for the battleship, she appeared because the fact that a Station in just this orbit was about to commence operations was news important enough to cross the Solar System and push through many strata of bureaucracy. The heads of the recently elected North American government became suddenly, fully aware of what had been going on.

Michael Blades was outside, overseeing the installation of a receptor, when his earplug buzzed. He thrust his chin against the tuning plate, switching from gang to interoffice band. "Mike?" said Avis Page's voice, "You're wanted up front."

"Now?" he objected. "Whatever for?"

"Courtesy visit from the NASS *Altair*. You've lost track of time, my boy."

"What the . . . the jumping blue blazes are you talking about? We've had our courtesy visit. Jimmy and I both went over to pay our respects, and we had Rear Admiral Hulse here to dinner. What more do they expect, for Harry's sake?"

"Don't you remember? Since there wasn't room to entertain his officers, you promised to take them on a personal guided tour later. I made the appointment the very next watch. Now's the hour."

"Oh, yes, it comes back to me. Yeah. Hulse brought a magnum of champagne with him, and after so long a time drinking recycled water, my capacity was shot to pieces. I got a warm glow of good fellowship on, and offered—Let Jimmy handle it, I'm busy."

"The party's too large, he says. You'll have to take half of them. Their gig will dock in thirty minutes."

"Well, depute somebody else."

"That'd be rude, Mike. Have you forgotten how sensitive they are about rank at home?" Avis hesitated. "If what I believe about the mood back there is true, we can use the good will of high-level Navy personnel. And any other influential people in sight."

Blades drew a deep breath. "You're too blinking sensible. Remind me to fire you after I've made my first ten million bucks."

"What'll you do for your next ten million, then?" snipped his secretary-file clerk-confidante-adviser-et cetera.

"Nothing. I'll just squander the first."

"Goody! Can I help?"

"Uh . . . I'll be right along." Blades switched off. His ears felt hot, as often of late when he tangled with Avis, and he unlimbered only a few choice oaths.

"Troubles?" asked Carlos Odonaju.

Blades stood a moment, looking around, before he answered. He was on the wide end of the Sword, which was shaped roughly like a truncated pyramid. Beyond him and his half dozen men stretched a vista of pitted rock, jutting crags, gulf-black shadows, under the glare of floodlamps. A few kilometers away, the farthest horizon ended, chopped off like a cliff. Beyond lay the stars, crowding that night which never ends. It grew very still while the gang waited for his word. He could listen to his own lungs and pulse, loud in the spacesuit; he could even notice its interior smell, blend of plastic and oxygen cycle chemicals, flesh and sweat. He was used to the sensation of hanging upside down on the surface, grip-soled boots holding him against that fractional gee by which the asteroid's rotation overcame its feeble gravity. But it came to him that this was an eerie bat-fashion way for an Oregon farm boy to stand.

Oregon was long behind him, though, not only the food factory where he grew up but the coasts where he had fished and the woods where he had tramped. No loss. There'd always been too many tourists. You couldn't escape from people on Earth. Cold and vacuum and raw rock and everything, the Belt was better. It annoyed him to be interrupted here.

Could Carlos take over as foreman? N-no, Blades decided, not yet. A gas receptor was an intricate piece of equipment. Carlos was a good man of his hands. Every one of the hundred-odd in the Station necessarily was. But he hadn't done this kind of work often enough.

"I have to quit," Blades said. "Secure the stuff and report back to Buck Meyers over at the dock, the lot of you. His crew's putting in another recoil pier, as I suppose you know. They'll find jobs for you. I'll see you here again on your next watch."

*

10

He waved—being half the nominal ownership of this place didn't justify snobbery, when everyone must work together or die—and stepped off toward the nearest entry lock with that flowing spaceman's pace which always keeps one foot on the ground. Even so, he didn't unshackle his inward-reeling lifeline till he was inside the chamber.

On the way he topped a gaunt ridge and had a clear view of the balloons that were attached to the completed receptors. Those that were still full bulked enormous, like ghostly moons. The Jovian gases that strained their tough elastomer did not much blur the stars seen through them; but they swelled high enough to catch the light of the hidden sun and shimmer with it. The nearly discharged balloons hung thin, straining outward. Two full ones passed in slow orbit against the constellations. They were waiting to be hauled in and coupled fast, to release their loads into the Station's hungry chemical plant. But there were not yet enough facilities to handle them at once—and the *Pallas Castle* would soon be arriving with another—Blades found that he needed a few extra curses.

Having cycled through the air lock, he removed his suit and stowed it, also the heavy gloves which kept him from frostbite as he touched its space-cold exterior. Tastefully clad in a Navy surplus Long John, he started down the corridors.

Now that the first stage of burrowing within the asteroid had been completed, most passages went through its body, rather than being plastic tubes snaking across the surface. Nothing had been done thus far about facing them. They were merely shafts, two meters square, lined with doorways, ventilator grilles, and fluoropanels. They had no thermocoils. Once the nickel-iron mass had been sufficiently warmed up, the waste heat of man and his industry kept it that way. The dark, chipped-out tunnels throbbed with machine noises. Here and there a girlie picture or a sentimental landscape from Earth was posted. Men moved busily along them, bearing tools, instruments, supplies. They were from numerous countries, those men, though mostly North Americans, but they had acquired a likeness, a rangy leathery look and a free-swinging stride, that went beyond their colorful coveralls.

"Hi, Mike . . . . How's she spinning? . . . Hey, Mike, you heard the latest story about the Martian and the bishop? . . . Can you spare me a minute? We got troubles in the separator manifolds . . . . What's the hurry, Mike, your batteries overcharged?" Blades waved the hails aside. There was need for haste. You could move fast indoors, under the low weight which became lower as you approached the axis of rotation, with no fear of tumbling off. But it was several kilometers from the gas receptor end to the people end of the asteroid.

He rattled down a ladder and entered his cramped office out of breath. Avis Page looked up from her desk and wrinkled her freckled snub nose at him. "You ought to take a shower, but there isn't time," she said. "Here, use my antistinker." She threw him a spray cartridge with a deft motion. "I got your suit and beardex out of your cabin."

"Have I no privacy?" he grumbled, but grinned in her direction. She wasn't much to look at—not ugly, just small, brunette, and unspectacular—but she was a supernova of an assistant. Make somebody a good wife some day. He wondered why she hadn't taken advantage of the situation here to snaffle a husband. A dozen women, all but two of them married, and a hundred men, was a ratio even more lopsided than the norm in the Belt. Of course with so much work to do, and with everybody conscious of the need to maintain cordial relations, sex didn't get much chance to rear its lovely head. Still—

She smiled back with the gentleness that he found disturbing when he noticed it. "Shoo," she said. "Your guests will be here any minute. You're to meet them in Jimmy's office."

*

Blades ducked into the tiny washroom. He wasn't any 3V star himself, he decided as he smeared cream over his face: big, homely, red-haired. *But not something you'd be scared to meet in a dark alley, either,* he added smugly. In fact, there had been an alley in Aresopolis . . . . Things were expected to be going so smoothly by the time they approached conjunction with Mars that he could run over to that sinful ginful city for a vacation. Long overdue . . . whooee! He wiped off his whiskers, shucked the zipskin, and climbed into the white pants and high-collared blue tunic that must serve as formal garb.

Emerging, he stopped again at Avis' desk. "Any message from the *Pallas*?" he asked.

"No," the girl said. "But she ought to be here in another two watches, right on sked. You worry too much, Mike."

"Somebody has to, and I haven't got Jimmy's Buddhist ride-with-the-punches attitude."

"You should cultivate it." She grew curious. The brown eyes lingered on him. "Worry's contagious. You make me fret about you."

"Nothing's going to give me an ulcer but the shortage of booze on this rock. Uh, if Bill Mbolo should call about those catalysts while I'm gone, tell him—" He ran off a string of instructions and headed for the door.

INDUSTRIAL REVOLUTION

Chung's hangout was halfway around the asteroid, so that one chief or the other could be a little nearer the scene of any emergency. Not that they spent much time at their desks. Shorthanded and undermechanized, they were forever having to help out in the actual construction. Once in a while Blades found himself harking wistfully back to his days as an engineer with Solar Metals: good pay, interesting if hazardous work on flying mountains where men had never trod before, and no further responsibilities. But most asterites had the dream of becoming their own bosses.

When he arrived, the *Altair* officers were already there, a score of correct young men in white dress uniforms. Short, squat, and placid looking, Jimmy Chung stood making polite conversation. "Ah, there," he said, "Lieutenant Ziska and gentlemen, my partner, Michael Blades, Mike, may I present—"

Blades' attention stopped at Lieutenant Ziska. He heard vaguely that she was the head quartermaster officer. But mainly she was tall and blond and blue-eyed, with a bewitching dimple when she smiled, and filled her gown the way a Cellini Venus doubtless filled its casting mold.

"Very pleased to meet you, Mr. Blades," she said as if she meant it. Maybe she did! He gulped for air.

"And Commander Leibknecht," Chung said across several light-years. "Commander Leibknecht. *Commander Leibknecht.*"

"Oh. Sure. 'Scuse." Blades dropped Lieutenant Ziska's hand in reluctant haste. "Hardjado, C'mander Leibfraumilch."

Somehow the introductions were gotten through. "I'm sorry we have to be so inhospitable," Chung said, "but you'll see how crowded we are. About all we can do is show you around, if you're interested."

"Of course you're interested," said Blades to Lieutenant Ziska. "I'll show you some gimmicks I thought up myself."

Chung scowled at him. "We'd best divide the party and proceed along alternate routes," he said, "We'll meet again in the mess for coffee, Lieutenant Ziska, would you like to—"

"Come with me? Certainly," Blades said.

Chung's glance became downright murderous. "I thought—" he began.

"Sure." Blades nodded vigorously. "You being the senior partner, you'll take the highest ranking of these gentlemen, and I'll be in Scotland before you. C'mon, let's get started. May I?" He offered the quartermistress his arm. She smiled and took it. He supposed that eight or ten of her fellows trailed them.

*

The first disturbing note was sounded on the verandah.

They had glanced at the cavelike dormitories where most of the personnel lived; at the recreation dome topside which made the life tolerable; at kitchen, sick bay, and the other service facilities; at the hydroponic tanks and yeast vats which supplied much of the Station's food; at the tiny cabins scooped out for the top engineers and the married couples. Before leaving this end of the asteroid, Blades took his group to the verandah. It was a clear dome jutting from the surface, softly lighted, furnished as a primitive officers' lounge, open to a view of half the sky.

"Oh-h," murmured Ellen Ziska. Unconsciously she moved closer to Blades.

Young Lieutenant Commander Gilbertson gave her a somewhat jaundiced look. "You've seen deep space often enough before," he said.

INDUSTRIAL REVOLUTION

"Through a port or a helmet." Her eyes glimmered enormous in the dusk. "Never like this."

The stars crowded close in their wintry myriads. The galactic belt glistened, diamond against infinite darkness. Vision toppled endlessly outward, toward the far mysterious shimmer of the Andromeda Nebula; silence was not a mere absence of noise, but a majestic presence, the seething of suns.

"What about the observation terrace at Leyburg?" Gilbertson challenged.

"That was different," Ellen Ziska said. "Everything was safe and civilized. This is like being on the edge of creation."

Blades could see why Goddard House had so long resisted the inclusion of female officers on ships of the line, despite political pressure at home and the Russian example abroad. He was glad they'd finally given in. Now if only he could build himself up as a dashing, romantic type . . . But how long would the *Altair* stay? Her stopover seemed quite extended already, for a casual visit in the course of a routine patrol cruise. He'd have to work fast.

"Yes, we are pretty isolated," he said. "The Jupiter ships just unload their balloons, pick up the empties, and head right back for another cargo."

"I don't understand how you can found an industry here, when your raw materials only arrive at conjunction," Ellen said.

"Things will be different once we're in full operation," Blades assured her. "Then we'll be doing enough business to pay for a steady input, transshipped from whatever depot is nearest Jupiter at any given time."

"You've actually built this simply to process . . . gas?" Gilbertson interposed. Blades didn't know whether he was being

16

sarcastic or asking a genuine question. It was astonishing how ignorant Earthsiders, even space-traveling Earthsiders, often were about such matters.

"Jovian gas is rich stuff," he explained. "Chiefly hydrogen and helium, of course; but the scoopships separate out most of that during a pickup. The rest is ammonia, water, methane, a dozen important organics, including some of the damn . . . doggonedest metallic complexes you ever heard of. We need them as the basis of a chemosynthetic industry, which we need for survival, which we need if we're to get the minerals that were the reason for colonizing the Belt in the first place." He waved his hand at the sky. "When we really get going, we'll attract settlement. This asteroid has companions, waiting for people to come and mine them. Homeships and orbital stations will be built. In ten years there'll be quite a little city clustered around the Sword."

"It's happened before," nodded tight-faced Commander Warburton of Gunnery Control.

"It's going to happen a lot oftener," Blades said enthusiastically. "The Belt's going to grow!" He aimed his words at Ellen. "This is the real frontier. The planets will never amount to much. It's actually harder to maintain human-type conditions on so big a mass, with a useless atmosphere around you, than on a lump in space like this. And the gravity wells are so deep. Even given nuclear power, the energy cost of really exploiting a planet is prohibitive. Besides which, the choice minerals are buried under kilometers of rock. On a metallic asteroid, you can find almost everything you want directly under your feet. No limit to what you can do."

"But your own energy expenditure—" Gilbertson objected.

INDUSTRIAL REVOLUTION

"That's no problem." As if on cue, the worldlet's spin brought the sun into sight. Tiny but intolerably brilliant, it flooded the dome with harsh radiance. Blades lowered the blinds on that side. He pointed in the opposite direction, toward several sparks of equal brightness that had manifested themselves.

"Hundred-meter parabolic mirrors," he said. "Easy to make; you spray a thin metallic coat on a plastic backing. They're in orbit around us, each with a small geegee unit to control drift and keep it aimed directly at the sun. The focused radiation charges heavy-duty accumulators, which we then collect and use for our power source in all our mobile work."

"Do you mean you haven't any nuclear generator?" asked Warburton.

He seemed curiously intent about it. Blades wondered why, but nodded. "That's correct. We don't want one. Too dangerous for us. Nor is it necessary. Even at this distance from the sun, and allowing for assorted inefficiencies, a mirror supplies better than five hundred kilowatts, twenty-four hours a day, year after year, absolutely free."

"Hm-m-m. Yes." Warburton's lean head turned slowly about, to rake Blades with a look of calculation. "I understand that's the normal power system in Stations of this type. But we didn't know if it was used in your case, too."

Why should you care? Blades thought.

He shoved aside his faint unease and urged Ellen toward the dome railing. "Maybe we can spot your ship, Lieutenant, uh, Miss Ziska. Here's a telescope. Let me see, her orbit ought to run about so . . . . "

*

He hunted until the *Altair* swam into the viewfield. At this distance the spheroid looked like a tiny crescent moon, dully painted; but he could make out the sinister shapes of a rifle turret and a couple of missile launchers. "Have a look," he invited. Her hair tickled his nose, brushing past him. It had a delightful sunny odor.

"How small she seems," the girl said, with the same note of wonder as before. "And how huge when you're aboard."

Big, all right, Blades knew, and loaded to the hatches with nuclear hellfire. But not massive. A civilian spaceship carried meteor plating, but since that was about as useful as wet cardboard against modern weapons, warcraft sacrificed it for the sake of mobility. The self-sealing hull was thin magnesium, the outer shell periodically renewed as cosmic sand eroded it.

"I'm not surprised we orbited, instead of docking," Ellen remarked. "We'd have butted against your radar and bellied into your control tower."

"Well, actually, no," said Blades. "Even half finished, our dock's big enough to accommodate you, as you'll see today. Don't forget, we anticipate a lot of traffic in the future. I'm puzzled why you didn't accept our invitation to use it."

"Doctrine!" Warburton clipped.

The sun came past the blind and touched the officers' faces with incandescence. Did some look startled, one or two open their mouths as if to protest and then snap them shut again at a warning look? Blades' spine tingled. *I never heard of any such doctrine,* he thought, *least of all when a North American ship drops in on a North American Station.*

"Is . . . er . . . is there some international crisis brewing?" he inquired.

"Why, no." Ellen straightened from the telescope. "I'd say relations have seldom been as good as they are now. What makes you ask?"

"Well, the reason your captain didn't—"

"Never mind," Warburton said. "We'd better continue the tour, if you please."

Blades filed his misgivings for later reference. He might have fretted immediately, but Ellen Ziska's presence forbade that. A sort of Pauli exclusion principle. One can't have two spins simultaneously, can one? He gave her his arm again. "Let's go on to Central Control," he proposed. "That's right behind the people section."

"You know, I can't get over it," she told him softly. "This miracle you've wrought. I've never been more proud of being human."

"Is this your first long space trip?"

"Yes, I was stationed at Port Colorado before the new Administration reshuffled armed service assignments."

"They did? How come?"

"I don't know. Well, that is, during the election campaign the Social Justice Party did talk a lot about old-line officers who were too hidebound to carry out modern policies effectively. But it sounded rather silly to me."

Warburton compressed his lips. "I do not believe it is proper for service officers to discuss political issues publicly," he said like a machine gun.

Ellen flushed. "S-sorry, commander."

Blades felt a helpless anger on her account. He wasn't sure why. What was she to him? He'd probably never see her again.

A hell of an attractive target, to be sure; and after so much celibacy he was highly vulnerable; but did she really matter?

He turned his back on Warburton and his eyes on her—a five thousand per cent improvement—and diverted her from her embarrassment by asking, "Are you from Colorado, then, Miss Ziska?"

"Oh, no. Toronto."

"How'd you happen to join the Navy, if I may make so bold?"

"Gosh, that's hard to say. But I guess mostly I felt so crowded at home. So, pigeonholed. The world seemed to be nothing but neat little pigeonholes."

"Uh-huh. Same here. I was also a square pigeon in a round hole." She laughed. "Luckily," he added, "Space is too big for compartments."

Her agreement lacked vigor. The Navy must have been a disappointment to her. But she couldn't very well say so in front of her shipmates.

Hm-m-m . . . if she could be gotten away from them—"How long will you be here?" he inquired. His pulse thuttered.

"We haven't been told," she said.

"Some work must be done on the missile launchers," Warburton said. "That's best carried out here, where extra facilities are available if we need them. Not that I expect we will." He paused. "I hope we won't interfere with your own operations."

"Far from it." Blades beamed at Ellen. "Or, more accurately, this kind of interference I don't mind in the least."

She blushed and her eyelids fluttered. Not that she was a fluffhead, he realized. But to avoid incidents, Navy regulations enforced an inhuman correctness between personnel of opposite sexes. After weeks in the black, meeting a man who could pay a compliment without risking court-martial must be like a shot of adrenalin. Better and better!

"Are you sure?" Warburton persisted. "For instance, won't we be in the way when the next ship comes from Jupiter?"

"She'll approach the opposite end of the asteroid," Blades said. "Won't stay long, either."

"How long?"

"One watch, so the crew can relax a bit among those of us who're off duty. It'd be a trifle longer if we didn't happen to have an empty bag at the moment. But never very long. Even running under thrust the whole distance, Jupe's a good ways off. They've no time to waste."

"When is the next ship due?"

"The *Pallas Castle* is expected in the second watch from now."

"Second watch. I see." Warburton stalked on with a brooding expression on his Puritan face.

*

Blades might have speculated about that, but someone asked him why the Station depended on spin for weight. Why not put in an internal field generator, like a ship? Blades explained patiently that an Emett large enough to produce uniform pull through a volume as big as the Sword was rather expensive. "Eventually, when we're a few megabucks ahead of the game—"

"Do you really expect to become rich?" Ellen asked. Her tone was awed. No Earthsider had that chance any more, except for the great corporations. "*Individually* rich?"

"We can't fail to. I tell you, this is a frontier like nothing since the Conquistadores. We could very easily have been wiped out in the first couple of years—financially or physically—by any of a thousand accidents. But now we're too far along for that. We've got it made, Jimmy and I."

"What will you do with your wealth?"

"Live like an old-time sultan," Blades grinned. Then, because it was true as well as because he wanted to shine in her eyes: "Mostly, though, we'll go on to new things. There's so much that needs to be done. Not simply more asteroid mines. We need farms; timber; parks; passenger and cargo liners; every sort of machine. I'd like to try getting at some of that water frozen in the Saturnian System. Altogether, I see no end to the jobs. It's no good our depending on Earth for anything. Too expensive, too chancy. The Belt has to be made completely self-sufficient."

"With a nice rakeoff for Sword Enterprises," Gilbertson scoffed.

"Why, sure. Aren't we entitled to some return?"

"Yes. But not so out of proportion as the Belt companies seem to expect. They're only using natural resources that rightly belong to the people, and the accumulated skills and wealth of an entire society."

"Huh! The People didn't do anything with the Sword. Jimmy and I and our boys did. No Society was around here grubbing nickel-iron and riding out gravel storms; we were."

"Let's leave politics alone," Warburton snapped. But it was mostly Ellen's look of distress which shut Blades up.

To everybody's relief, they reached Central Control about then. It was a complex of domes and rooms, crammed with more equipment than Blades could put a name to. Computers were in Chung's line, not his. He wasn't able to answer all of Warburton's disconcertingly sharp questions.

INDUSTRIAL REVOLUTION

But in a general way he could. Whirling through vacuum with a load of frail humans and intricate artifacts, the Sword must be at once machine, ecology, and unified organism. Everything had to mesh. A failure in the thermodynamic balance, a miscalculation in supply inventory, a few mirrors perturbed out of proper orbit, might spell Ragnarok. The chemical plant's purifications and syntheses were already a network too large for the human mind to grasp as a whole, and it was still growing. Even where men could have taken charge, automation was cheaper, more reliable, less risky of lives. The computer system housed in Central Control was not only the brain, but the nerves and heart of the Sword.

"Entirely cryotronic, eh?" Warburton commented. "That seems to be the usual practice at the Stations. Why?"

"The least expensive type for us," Blades answered. "There's no problem in maintaining liquid helium here."

Warburton's gaze was peculiarly intense. "Cryotronic systems are vulnerable to magnetic and radiation disturbances."

"Uh-huh. That's one reason we don't have a nuclear power plant. This far from the sun, we don't get enough emission to worry about. The asteroid's mass screens out what little may arrive. I know the TIMM system is used on ships; but if nothing else, the initial cost is more than we want to pay."

"What's TIMM?" inquired the *Altair's* chaplain.

"Thermally Integrated Micro-Miniaturized," Ellen said crisply. "Essentially, ultraminiaturized ceramic-to-metal-seal vacuum tubes running off thermionic generators. They're immune to gamma ray and magnetic pulses, easily shielded against particle radiation, and economical of power." She grinned. "Don't tell me there's nothing about them in Leviticus, Padre!"

"Very fine for a ship's autopilot," Blades agreed. "But as I said, we needn't worry about rad or mag units here, we don't mind sprawling a bit, and as for thermal efficiency, we want to waste some heat. It goes to maintain internal temperature."

"In other words, efficiency depends on what you need to effish," Ellen bantered. She grew grave once more and studied him for a while before she mused, "The same person who swung a pick, a couple of years ago, now deals with something as marvelous as this . . . . " He forgot about worrying.

*

But he remembered later, when the gig had left and Chung called him to his office. Avis came too, by request. As she entered, she asked why.

"You were visiting your folks Earthside last year," Chung said. "Nobody else in the Station has been back as recently as that."

"What can I tell you?"

"I'm not sure. Background, perhaps. The feel of the place. We don't really know, out in the Belt, what's going on there. The beamcast news is hardly a trickle. Besides, you have more common sense in your left little toe than that big mick yonder has on his entire copperplated head."

They seated themselves in the cobwebby low-gee chairs around Chung's desk. Blades took out his pipe and filled the bowl with his tobacco ration for today. Wouldn't it be great, he thought dreamily, if this old briar turned out to be an Aladdin's lamp, and the smoke condensed into a blonde she-Canadian—?

"Wake up, will you?" Chung barked.

"Huh?" Blades started. "Oh. Sure. What's the matter? You look like a fish on Friday."

"Maybe with reason. Did you notice anything unusual with that party you were escorting?"

"Yes, indeed."

"What?"

"About one hundred seventy-five centimeters tall, yellow hair, blue eyes, and some of the smoothest fourth-order curves I ever—"

"Mike, stop that!" Avis sounded appalled. "This is serious."

"I agree. She'll be leaving in a few more watches."

The girl bit her lip. "You're too old for that mooncalf rot and you know it."

"Agreed again. I feel more like a bull." Blades made pawing motions on the desktop.

"There's a lady present," Chung said.

Blades saw that Avis had gone quite pale. "I'm sorry," he blurted. "I never thought . . . I mean, you've always seemed like—"

"One of the boys," she finished for him in a brittle tone. "Sure. Forget it. What's the problem, Jimmy?"

Chung folded his hands and stared at them. "I can't quite define that," he answered, word by careful word. "Perhaps I've simply gone spacedizzy. But when we called on Admiral Hulse, and later when he called on us, didn't you get the impression of, well, wariness? Didn't he seem to be watching and probing, every minute we were together?"

"I wouldn't call him a cheerful sort," Blades nodded. "Stiff as molasses on Pluto. But I suppose . . . supposed he's just naturally that way."

Chung shook his head. "It wasn't a normal standoffishness. You've heard me reminisce about the time I was on Vesta with the North American technical representative, when the Convention was negotiated."

"Yes, I've heard that story a few times," said Avis dryly.

"Remember, that was right after the Europa Incident. We'd come close to a space war—undeclared, but it would have been nasty. We were still close. Every delegate went to that conference cocked and primed.

"Hulse had the same manner."

*

A silence fell. Blades said at length, "Well, come to think of it, he did ask some rather odd questions. He seemed to twist the conversation now and then, so he could find things out like our exact layout, emergency doctrine, and so forth. It didn't strike me as significant, though."

"Nor me," Chung admitted. "Taken in isolation, it meant nothing. But these visitors today—Sure, most of them obviously didn't suspect anything untoward. But that Liebknecht, now. Why was he so interested in Central Control? Nothing new or secret there. Yet he kept asking for details like the shielding factor of the walls."

"So did Commander Warburton," Blades remembered. "Also, he wanted to know exactly when the *Pallas* is due, how long she'll stay . . . hm-m-m, yes, whether we have any radio linkage with the outside, like to Ceres or even the nearest Commission base—"

"Did you tell him that we don't?" Avis asked sharply.

"Yes. Shouldn't I have?"

"It scarcely makes any difference," Chung said in a resigned voice. "As thoroughly as they went over the ground, they'd have seen what we do and do not have installed so far."

He leaned forward. "Why are they hanging around?" he asked. "I was handed some story about overhauling the missile system."

"Me, too," Blades said.

"But you don't consider a job complete till it's been tested. And you don't fire a test shot, even a dummy, this close to a Station. Besides, what could have gone wrong? I can't see a ship departing Earth orbit for a long cruise without everything being in order. And they didn't mention any meteorites, any kind of trouble, en route. Furthermore, why do the work here? The Navy yard's at Ceres. We can't spare them any decent amount of materials or tools or help."

Blades frowned. His own half-formulated doubts shouldered to the fore, which was doubly unpleasant after he'd been considering Ellen Ziska. "They tell me the international situation at home is O.K.," he offered.

Avis nodded. "What newsfaxes we get in the mail indicate as much," she said. "So why this hanky-panky?" After a moment, in a changed voice: "Jimmy, you begin to scare me a little."

"I scare myself," Chung said.

"Every morning when you debeard," Blades said; but his heart wasn't in it. He shook himself and protested: "Damnation, they're our own countrymen. We're engaged in a lawful business. Why should they do anything to us?"

"Maybe Avis can throw some light on that," Chung suggested.

The girl twisted her fingers together. "Not me," she said. "I'm no politician."

"But you were home not so long ago. You talked with people, read the news, watched the 3V. Can't you at least give an impression?"

"N-no—Well, of course the preliminary guns of the election campaign were already being fired. The Social Justice Party was talking a lot about . . . oh, it seemed so ridiculous that I didn't pay much attention."

"They talked about how the government had been pouring billions and billions of dollars into space, while overpopulation produced crying needs in America's back yard," Chung said. "We know that much, even in the Belt. We know the appropriations are due to be cut, now the Essjays are in. So what?"

"We don't need a subsidy any longer," Blades remarked. "It'd help a lot, but we can get along without if we have to, and personally, I prefer that. Less government money means less government control."

"Sure," Avis said. "There was more than that involved, however. The Essjays were complaining about the small return on the investment. Not enough minerals coming back to Earth."

"Well, for Jupiter's sake," Blades exclaimed, "what do they expect? We have to build up our capabilities first."

"They even said, some of them, that enough reward never would be gotten. That under existing financial policies, the Belt would go in for its own expansion, use nearly everything it produced for itself and export only a trickle to America. I had to explain to several of my parents' friends that I wasn't really a socially irresponsible capitalist."

"Is that all the information you have?" Chung asked when she fell silent.

"I . . . I suppose so. Everything was so vague. No dramatic events. More of an atmosphere than a concrete thing."

INDUSTRIAL REVOLUTION

*

"Still, you confirm my own impression," Chung said. Blades jerked his undisciplined imagination back from the idea of a Thing, with bug eyes and tentacles, cast in reinforced concrete, and listened as his partner summed up:

"The popular feeling at home has turned against private enterprise. You can hardly call a corporate monster like Systemic Developments a private enterprise! The new President and Congress share that mood. We can expect to see it manifested in changed laws and regulations. But what has this got to do with a battleship parked a couple of hundred kilometers from us?"

"If the government doesn't want the asterites to develop much further—" Blades bit hard on his pipestem. "They must know we have a caviar mine here. We'll be the only city in this entire sector."

"But we're still a baby," Avis said. "We won't be important for years to come. Who'd have it in for a baby?"

"Besides, we're Americans, too," Chung said. "If that were a foreign ship, the story might be different—Wait a minute! Could they be thinking of establishing a new base here?"

"The Convention wouldn't allow," said Blades.

"Treaties can always be renegotiated, or even denounced. But first you have to investigate quietly, find out if it's worth your while."

"Hoo hah, what lovely money that'd mean!"

"And lovely bureaucrats crawling out of every file cabinet," Chung said grimly. "No, thank you. We'll fight any such attempt to the last lawyer. We've got a good basis, too, in our charter. If the suit is tried on Ceres, as I believe it has to be, we'll get a sympathetic court as well."

"Unless they ring in an Earthside judge," Avis warned.

"Yeah, that's possible. Also, they could spring proceedings on us without notice. We've got to find out in advance, so we can prepare. Any chance of pumping some of those officers?"

"'Fraid not," Avis said. "The few who'd be in the know are safely back on shipboard."

"We could invite 'em here individually," said Blades. "As a matter of fact, I already have a date with Lieutenant Ziska."

"What?" Avis' mouth fell open.

"Yep," Blades said complacently. "End of the next watch, so she can observe the *Pallas* arriving. I'm to fetch her on a scooter." He blew a fat smoke ring. "Look, Jimmy, can you keep everybody off the porch for a while then? Starlight, privacy, soft music on the piccolo—who knows what I might find out?"

"You won't get anything from *her*," Avis spat. "No secrets or, or anything."

"Still, I look forward to making the attempt. C'mon, pal, pass the word. I'll do as much for you sometime."

"Times like that never seem to come for me," Chung groaned.

"Oh, let him play around with his suicide blonde," Avis said furiously. "We others have work to do. I . . . I'll tell you what, Jimmy. Let's not eat in the mess tonight. I'll draw our rations and fix us something special in your cabin."

*

A scooter was not exactly the ideal steed for a knight to convey his lady. It amounted to little more than three saddles and a locker, set atop an accumulator-powered gyrogravitic engine, sufficient to lift you off an asteroid and run at low acceleration. There were no navigating instruments. You locked the autopilot's radar-gravitic sensors onto your target object and it took you there, avoiding any bits of debris which might pass near; but you must watch the distance indicator and press the deceleration switch in time. If the 'pilot was turned off, free maneuver became possible, but that was a dangerous thing to try before you were almost on top of your destination. Stereoscopic vision fails beyond six or seven meters, and the human organism isn't equipped to gauge cosmic momenta.

Nevertheless, Ellen was enchanted. "This is like a dream," her voice murmured in Blades' earplug. "The whole universe, on every side of us. I could almost reach out and pluck those stars."

"You must have trained in powered spacesuits at the Academy," he said for lack of a more poetic rejoinder.

"Yes, but that's not the same. We had to stay near Luna's night side, to be safe from solar particles, and it bit a great chunk out of the sky. And then everything was so—regulated, disciplined—we did what we were ordered to do, and that was that. Here I feel free. You can't imagine how free." Hastily: "Do you use this machine often?"

"Well, yes, we have about twenty scooters at the Station. They're the most convenient way of flitting with a load: out to the mirrors to change accumulators, for instance, or across to one of the companion rocks where we're digging some ores that the Sword doesn't have. That kind of work." Blades would frankly rather have had her behind him on a motorskimmer, hanging on as they careened through a springtime countryside. He was glad when they reached the main forward air lock and debarked.

He was still gladder when the suits were off. Lieutenant Ziska in dress uniform was stunning, but Ellen in civvies, a fluffy low-cut blouse and close-fitting slacks, was a hydrogen blast. He wanted to roll over and pant, but settled for saying, "Welcome back" and holding her hand rather longer than necessary.

With a shy smile, she gave him a package. "I drew this before leaving," she said. "I thought, well, your life is so austere—"

"A demi of Sandeman," he said reverently. "I won't tell you you shouldn't have, but I will tell you you're a sweet girl."

"No, really." She flushed. "After we've put you to so much trouble."

"Let's go crack this," he said. "The *Pallas* has called in, but she won't be visible for a while yet."

*

They made their way to the verandah, picking up a couple of glasses enroute. Bless his envious heart, Jimmy had warned the other boys off as requested. *I hope Avis cooks him a Cordon Bleu dinner*, Blades thought. *Nice kid, Avis, if she'd quit trying to . . . what? . . . mother me?* He forgot about her, with Ellen to seat by the rail.

The Milky Way turned her hair frosty and glowed in her eyes. Blades poured the port with much ceremony and raised his glass. "Here's to your frequent return," he said.

Her pleasure dwindled a bit. "I don't know if I should drink to that. We aren't likely to be back, ever."

"Drink anyway. Gling, glang, gloria!" The rims tinkled together. "After all," said Blades, "this isn't the whole universe. We'll both be getting around. See you on Luna?"

"Maybe."

He wondered if he was pushing matters too hard. She didn't look at ease. "Oh, well," he said, "if nothing else, this has been a grand break in the monotony for us. I don't wish the Navy ill, but if trouble had to develop, I'm thankful it developed here."

"Yes—"

"How's the repair work progressing? Slowly, I hope."

"I don't know."

"You should have some idea, being in QM."

"No supplies have been drawn."

Blades stiffened.

"What's the matter?" Ellen sounded alarmed.

"Huh?" *A fine conspirator I make, if she can see my emotions on me in neon capitals!* "Nothing. Nothing. It just seemed a little strange, you know. Not taking any replacement units."

"I understand the work is only a matter of making certain adjustments."

"Then they should've finished a lot quicker, shouldn't they?"

"Please," she said unhappily. "Let's not talk about it. I mean, there are such things as security regulations."

Blades gave up on that tack. But Chung's idea might be worth probing a little. "Sure," he said. "I'm sorry, I didn't mean to pry." He took another sip as he hunted for suitable words. A beautiful girl, a golden wine . . . and vice versa . . . why couldn't he simply relax and enjoy himself? Did he have to go fretting about what was probably a perfectly harmless conundrum? . . . Yes. However, recreation might still combine with business.

"Permit me to daydream," he said, leaning close to her. "The Navy's going to establish a new base here, and the *Altair* will be assigned to it."

"Daydream indeed!" she laughed, relieved to get back to a mere flirtation. "Ever hear about the Convention of Vesta?"

"Treaties can be renegotiated," Blades plagiarized.

"What do we need an extra base for? Especially since the government plans to spend such large sums on social welfare. They certainly don't want to start an arms race besides."

*

Blades nodded. *Jimmy's notion did seem pretty thin*, he thought with a slight chill, *and now I guess it's completely whiffed.* Mostly to keep the conversation going, he shrugged and said, "My partner—and me, too, aside from the privilege of your company—wouldn't have wanted it anyhow. Not that we're unpatriotic, but there are plenty of other potential bases, and we'd rather keep government agencies out of here."

"Can you, these days?"

"Pretty much. We're under a new type of charter, as a private partnership. The first such charter in the Belt, as far as I know, though there'll be more in the future. The Bank of Ceres financed us. We haven't taken a nickel of federal money."

"Is that possible?"

"Just barely. I'm no economist, but I can see how it works. Money represents goods and labor. Hitherto those have been in mighty short supply out here. Government subsidies made up the difference, enabling us to buy from Earth. But now the asterites have built up enough population and industry that they have some capital surplus of their own, to invest in projects like this."

"Even so, frankly, I'm surprised that two men by themselves could get such a loan. It must be huge. Wouldn't the bank rather have lent the money to some corporation?"

"To tell the truth, we have friends who pulled wires for us. Also, it was done partly on ideological grounds. A lot of asterites would like to see more strictly home-grown enterprises, not committed to anyone on Earth. That's the only way we can grow. Otherwise our profits—our net production, that is—will continue to be siphoned off for the mother country's benefit."

"Well," Ellen said with some indignation, "that was the whole reason for planting asteroid colonies. You can't expect us to set you up in business, at enormous cost to ourselves—things we might have done at home—and get nothing but 'Ta' in return."

"Never fear, we'll repay you with interest," Blades said. "But whatever we make from our own work, over and above that, ought to stay here with us."

She grew angrier. "Your kind of attitude is what provoked the voters to elect Social Justice candidates."

"Nice name, that," mused Blades. "Who can be against social justice? But you know, I think I'll go into politics myself. I'll organize the North American Motherhood Party."

"You wouldn't be so flippant if you'd go see how people have to live back there."

"As bad as here? *Whew!*"

"Nonsense. You know that isn't true. But bad enough. And you aren't going to stick in these conditions. Only a few hours ago, you were bragging about the millions you intend to make."

"Millions *and* millions, if my strength holds out," leered Blades, thinking of the alley in Aresopolis. But he decided that that was then and Ellen was now, and what had started as a promising little party was turning into a dismal argument about politics.

"Let's not fight," he said. "We've got different orientations, and we'd only make each other mad. Let's discuss our next bottle instead . . . at the Coq d'Or in Paris, shall we say? Or Morraine's in New York."

She calmed down, but her look remained troubled. "You're right, we are different," she said low. "Isolated, living and working under conditions we can hardly imagine on Earth—and you can't really imagine our problems—yes, you're becoming another people. I hope it will never go so far that—No. I don't want to think about it." She drained her glass and held it out for a refill, smiling. "Very well, sir, when do you next plan to be in Paris?"

*

An exceedingly enjoyable while later, the time came to go watch the *Pallas Castle* maneuver in. In fact, it had somehow gotten past that time, and they were late; but they didn't hurry their walk aft. Blades took Ellen's hand; and she raised no objection. Schoolboyish, no doubt—however, he had reached the reluctant conclusion that for all his dishonorable intentions, this affair wasn't likely to go beyond the schoolboy stage. Not that he wouldn't keep trying.

As they glided through the refining and synthesizing section, which filled the broad half of the asteroid, the noise of pumps and regulators rose until it throbbed in their bones. Ellen gestured at one of the pipes which crossed the corridor overhead. "Do you really handle that big a volume at a time?" she asked above the racket.

"No," he said. "Didn't I explain before? The pipe's thick because it's so heavily armored."

"I'm glad you don't use that dreadful word 'cladded.' But why the armor? High pressure?"

"Partly. Also, there's an inertrans lining. Jupiter gas is hellishly reactive at room temperature. The metallic complexes especially; but think what a witch's brew the stuff is in every respect. Once it's been refined, of course, we have less trouble. That particular pipe is carrying it raw."

They left the noise behind and passed on to the approach control dome at the receptor end. The two men on duty glanced up and immediately went back to their instruments. Radio voices were staccato in the air. Blades led Ellen to an observation port.

She drew a sharp breath. Outside, the broken ground fell away to space and the stars. The ovoid that was the ship hung against them, lit by the hidden sun, a giant even at her distance but dwarfed by the balloon she towed. As that bubble tried ponderously to rotate, rainbow gleams ran across it, hiding and then revealing the constellations. Here, on the asteroid's axis, there was no weight, and one moved with underwater smoothness, as if disembodied. "Oh, a fairy tale," Ellen sighed.

Four sparks flashed out of the boat blisters along the ship's hull. "Scoopships," Blades told her. "They haul the cargo in, being so much more maneuverable. Actually, though, the mother vessel is going to park her load in orbit, while those boys bring in another one . . . see, there it comes into sight. We still haven't got the capacity to keep up with our deliveries."

"How many are there? Scoopships, that is."

"Twenty, but you don't need more than four for this job. They've got terrific power. Have to, if they're to dive from orbit down into the Jovian atmosphere, ram themselves full of gas, and come back. There they go."

The *Pallas Castle* was wrestling the great sphere she had hauled from Jupiter into a stable path computed by Central Control. Meanwhile the scoopships, small only by comparison with her, locked onto the other balloon as it drifted close. Energy poured into their drive fields. Spiraling downward, transparent globe and four laboring spacecraft vanished behind the horizon. The *Pallas* completed her own task, disengaged her towbars, and dropped from view, headed for the dock.

The second balloon rose again, like a huge glass moon on the opposite side of the Sword. Still it grew in Ellen's eyes, kilometer by kilometer of approach. So much mass wasn't easily handled, but the braking curve looked disdainfully smooth. Presently she could make out the scoopships in detail, elongated teardrops with the intake gates yawning in the blunt forward end, cockpit canopies raised very slightly above.

Instructions rattled from the men in the dome. The balloon veered clumsily toward the one free receptor. A derricklike structure released one end of a cable, which streamed skyward. Things that Ellen couldn't quite follow in this tricky light were done by the four tugs, mechanisms of their own extended to make their tow fast to the cable.

They did not cast loose at once, but continued to drag a little, easing the impact of centrifugal force. Nonetheless a slight shudder went through the dome as slack was taken up. Then the job was over. The scoopships let go and flitted off to join their mother vessel. The balloon was winched inward. Spacesuited men moved close, preparing to couple valves together.

"And eventually," Blades said into the abrupt quietness, "that cargo will become food, fabric, vitryl, plastiboard, reagents, fuels, a hundred different things. That's what we're here for."

"I've never seen anything so wonderful," Ellen said raptly. He laid an arm around her waist.

The intercom chose that precise moment to blare: "Attention! Emergency! All hands to emergency stations! Blades, get to Chung's office on the double! All hands to emergency stations!"

Blades was running before the siren had begun to howl.

Rear Admiral Barclay Hulse had come in person. He stood as if on parade, towering over Chung. The asterite was red with fury. Avis Page crouched in a corner, her eyes terrified.

Blades barreled through the doorway and stopped hardly short of a collision. "What's the matter?" he puffed.

"Plenty!" Chung snarled. "These incredible thumble-fumbed oafs—" His voice broke. *When he gets mad, it means something!*

Hulse nailed Blades with a glance. "Good day, sir," he clipped. "I have had to report a regrettable accident which will require you to evacuate the Station. Temporarily, I hope."

"Huh?"

"As I told Mr. Chung and Miss Page, a nuclear missile has escaped us. If it explodes, the radiation will be lethal, even in the heart of the asteroid."

"What . . . what—" Blades could only gobble at him.

"Fortunately, the *Pallas Castle* is here. She can take your whole complement aboard and move to a safe distance while we search for the object."

"How the *devil?*"

Hulse allowed himself a look of exasperation. "Evidently I'll have to repeat myself to you. Very well. You know we have had to make some adjustments on our launchers. What you did not know was the reason. Under the circumstances, I think it's permissible to tell you that several of them have a new and secret, experimental control system. One of our missions on this cruise was to carry out field tests. Well, it turned out that the system is still full of, ah, bugs. Gunnery Command has had endless trouble with it, has had to keep tinkering the whole way from Earth.

"Half an hour ago, while Commander Warburton was completing a reassembly—lower ranks aren't allowed in the test turrets—something happened. I can't tell you my guess as to what, but if you want to imagine that a relay got stuck, that will do for practical purposes. A missile was released under power. Not a dummy—the real thing. And release automatically arms the war head."

*

The news was like a hammerblow. Blades spoke an obscenity. Sweat sprang forth under his arms and trickled down his ribs.

"No such thing was expected," Hulse went on. "It's an utter disaster, and the designers of the system aren't likely to get any more contracts. But as matters were, no radar fix was gotten on it, and it was soon too far away for gyrogravitic pulse detection. The thrust vector is unknown. It could be almost anywhere now.

"Well, naval missiles are programmed to reverse acceleration if they haven't made a target within a given time. This one should be back in less than six hours. If it first detects our ship, everything is all right. It has optical recognition circuits that identify any North American warcraft by type, disarm the war head, and steer it home. But, if it first comes within fifty kilometers of some other mass—like this asteroid or one of the companion rocks—it will detonate. We'll make every effort to intercept, but space is big. You'll have to take your people to a safe distance. They can come back even after a blast, of course. There's no concussion in vacuum, and the fireball won't reach here. It's principally an anti-personnel weapon. But you must not be within the lethal radius of radiation."

"The hell we can come back!" Avis cried.

"I beg your pardon?" Hulse said.

"You imbecile! Don't you know Central Control here is cryotronic?"

Hulse did not flicker an eyelid. "So it is," he said expressionlessly. "I had forgotten."

*

Blades mastered his own shock enough to grate: "Well, we sure haven't. If that thing goes off, the gamma burst will kick up so many minority carriers in the transistors that the p-type crystals will act n-type, and the n-type act p-type, for a whole couple of microseconds. Every one of 'em will flip simultaneously! The computers' memory and program data systems will be scrambled beyond hope of reorganization."

"Magnetic pulse, too," Chung said. "The fireball plasma will be full of inhomogeneities moving at several per cent of light speed. Their electromagnetic output, hitting our magnetic core units, will turn them from super to ordinary conduction. Same effect, total computer amnesia. We haven't got enough shielding against it. Your TIMM systems can take that kind of a beating. Ours can't!"

"Very regrettable," Hulse said. "You'd have to reprogram everything—"

"Reprogram what?" Avis retorted. Tears started forth in her eyes. "We've told you what sort of stuff our chemical plant is handling. We can't shut it down on that short notice. It'll run wild. There'll be sodium explosions, hydrogen and organic combustion, n-n-nothing left here but wreckage!"

Hulse didn't unbend a centimeter. "I offer my most sincere apologies. If actual harm does occur, I'm sure the government will indemnify you. And, of course, my command will furnish what supplies may be needed for the *Pallas Castle* to transport you to the nearest Commission base. At the moment, though, you can do nothing but evacuate and hope we will be able to intercept the missile."

Blades knotted his fists. A sudden comprehension rushed up in him and he bellowed, "There isn't going to be an interception! This wasn't an accident!"

Hulse backed a step and drew himself even straighter. "Don't get overwrought," he advised.

"You louse-bitten, egg-sucking, bloated faggot-porter! How stupid do you think we are? As stupid as your Essjay bosses? By heaven, we're staying! Then see if you have the nerve to murder a hundred people!"

"Mike . . . Mike—" Avis caught his arm.

Hulse turned to Chung. "I'll overlook that unseemly outburst," he said. "But in light of my responsibilities and under the provisions of the Constitution, I am hereby putting this asteroid under martial law. You will have all personnel aboard the *Pallas Castle* and at a minimum distance of a thousand kilometers within four hours of this moment, or be subject to arrest and trial. Now I have to get back and commence operations. The *Altair* will maintain radio contact with you.

43

Good day." He bowed curtly, spun on his heel, and clacked from the room.

Blades started to charge after him. Chung caught his free arm. Together he and Avis dragged him to a stop. He stood cursing the air ultraviolet until Ellen entered.

"I couldn't keep up with you," she panted. "What's happened, Mike?"

The strength drained from Blades. He slumped into a chair and covered his face.

*

Chung explained in a few harsh words. "Oh-h-h," Ellen gasped. She went to Blades and laid her hands on his shoulders. "My poor Mike!"

After a moment she looked at the others. "I should report back, of course," she said, "but I won't be able to before the ship accelerates. So I'll have to stay with you till afterward. Miss Page, we left about half a bottle of wine on the verandah. I think it would be a good idea if you went and got it."

Avis bridled. "And why not you?"

"This is no time for personalities," Chung said. "Go on, Avis. You can be thinking what records and other paper we should take, while you're on your way. I've got to organize the evacuation. As for Miss Ziska, well, Mike needs somebody to pull him out of his dive."

"Her?" Avis wailed, and fled.

Chung sat down and flipped his intercom to Phone Central. "Get me Captain Janichevski aboard the *Pallas*," he ordered. "Hello, Adam? About that general alarm—"

Blades raised a haggard countenance toward Ellen's. "You better clear out, along with the women and any men who don't want to stay," he said. "But I think most of them will take the chance. They're on a profit-sharing scheme, they stand to lose too much if the place is ruined."

"What do you mean?"

"It's a gamble, but I don't believe Hulse's sealed orders extend to murder. If enough of us stay put, he'll have to catch that thing. He jolly well knows its exact trajectory."

"You forget we're under martial law," Chung said, aside to him. "If we don't go freely, he'll land some PP's and march us off at gunpoint. There isn't any choice. We've had the course."

"I don't understand," Ellen said shakily.

Chung went back to his intercom. Blades fumbled out his pipe and rolled it empty between his hands. "That missile was shot off on purpose," he said.

"What? No, you must be sick, that's impossible!"

"I realize you didn't know about it. Only three or four officers have been told. The job had to be done very, very secretly, or there'd be a scandal, maybe an impeachment. But it's still sabotage."

She shrank from him. "You're not making sense."

"Their own story doesn't make sense. It's ridiculous. A new missile system wouldn't be sent on a field trial clear to the Belt before it'd had enough tests closer to home to get the worst bugs out. A war-head missile wouldn't be stashed anywhere near something so unreliable, let alone be put under its control. The testing ship wouldn't hang around a civilian Station while her gunnery chief tinkered. And Hulse, Warburton, Liebknecht, they were asking in *such* detail about how radiation-proof we are."

"I can't believe it. Nobody will."

INDUSTRIAL REVOLUTION

"Not back home. Communication with Earth is so sparse and garbled. The public will only know there was an accident; who'll give a hoot about the details? We couldn't even prove anything in an asteroid court. The Navy would say, 'Classified information!' and that'd stop the proceedings cold. Sure, there'll be a board of inquiry—composed of naval officers. Probably honorable men, too. But what are they going to believe, the sworn word of their Goddard House colleague, or the rantings of an asterite bum?"

"Mike, I know this is terrible for you, but you've let it go to your head." Ellen laid a hand over his. "Suppose the worst happens. You'll be compensated for your loss."

"Yeah. To the extent of our personal investment. The Bank of Ceres still has nearly all the money that was put in. We didn't figure to have them paid off for another ten years. They, or their insurance carrier, will get the indemnity. And after our fiasco, they won't make us a new loan. They were just barely talked into it, the first time around. I daresay Systemic Developments will make them a nice juicy offer to take this job over."

Ellen colored. She stamped her foot. "You're talking like a paranoiac. Do you really believe the government of North America would send a battleship clear out here to do you dirt?"

"Not the whole government. A few men in the right positions is all that's necessary. I don't know if Hulse was bribed or talked into this. But probably he agreed as a duty. He's the prim type."

"A duty—to destroy a North American business?"

*

Chung finished at the intercom in time to answer: "Not permanent physical destruction, Miss Ziska. As Mike suggested, some corporation will doubtless inherit the Sword and repair the damage. But a private, purely asterite business . . . yes, I'm afraid Mike's right. We are the target."

"In mercy's name, why?"

"From the highest motives, of course," Chung sneered bitterly. "You know what the Social Justice Party thinks of private capitalism. What's more important, though, is that the Sword is the first Belt undertaking not tied to Mother Earth's apron strings. We have no commitments to anybody back there. We can sell our output wherever we like. It's notorious that the asterites are itching to build up their own self-sufficient industries. Quite apart from sentiment, we can make bigger profits in the Belt than back home, especially when you figure the cost of sending stuff in and out of Earth's gravitational well. So certainly we'd be doing most of our business out here.

"Our charter can't simply be revoked. First a good many laws would have to be revised, and that's politically impossible. There is still a lot of individualist sentiment in North America, as witness the fact that businesses do get launched and that the Essjays did have a hard campaign to get elected. What the new government wants is something like the Eighteenth Century English policy toward America. Keep the colonies as a source of raw materials and as a market for manufactured goods, but don't let them develop a domestic industry. You can't come right out and say that, but you can let the situation develop naturally.

"Only . . . here the Sword is, obviously bound to grow rich and expand in every direction. If we're allowed to develop, to reinvest our profits, we'll become the nucleus of independent asterite enterprise. If, on the other hand, we're wiped out by an unfortunate accident, there's no nucleus; and a small change in the banking laws is all that's needed to prevent others from getting started. Q.E.D."

"I daresay Hulse does think he's doing his patriotic duty," said Blades. "He wants to guarantee North America our natural resources—in the long run, maybe, our allegiance. If he has to commit sabotage, too bad, but it won't cost him any sleep."

"No!" Ellen almost screamed.

Chung sagged in his chair. "We're very neatly trapped," he said like an old man. "I don't see any way out. Think you can get to work now, Mike? You can assign group leaders for the evacuation—"

Blades jumped erect. "I can fight!" he growled.

"With what? Can openers?"

"You mean you're going to lie down and let them break us?"

Avis came back. She thrust the bottle into Blades' hands as he paced the room. "Here you are," she said in a distant voice.

He held it out toward Ellen. "Have some," he invited.

"Not with you . . . you subversive!"

Avis brightened noticeably, took the bottle and raised it. "Then here's to victory," she said, drank, and passed it to Blades.

He started to gulp; but the wine was too noble, and he found himself savoring its course down his throat. *Why*, he thought vaguely, *do people always speak with scorn about Dutch courage? The Dutch have real guts. They fought themselves free of Spain and free of the ocean itself; when the French or Germans came, they made the enemy sea their ally—*

The bottle fell from his grasp. In the weak acceleration, it hadn't hit the floor when Avis rescued it. "Gimme that, you big butterfingers," she exclaimed. Her free hand clasped his arm.

"Whatever happens, Mike," she said to him, "we're not quitting."

Still Blades stared beyond her. His fists clenched and unclenched. The noise of his breathing filled the room. Chung looked around in bewilderment; Ellen watched with waxing horror; Avis' eyes kindled.

"Holy smoking seegars," Blades whispered at last. "I really think we can swing it."

Captain Janichevski recoiled. "You're out of your skull!"

"Probably," said Blades. "Fun, huh?"

"You can't do this."

"We can try."

"Do you know what you're talking about? Insurrection, that's what. Quite likely piracy. Even if your scheme worked, you'd spend the next ten years in Rehab—at least."

"Maybe, provided the matter ever came to trial. But it won't."

"That's what you think. You're asking me to compound the felony, and misappropriate the property of my owners to boot." Janichevski shook his head. "Sorry, Mike. I'm sorry as hell about this mess. But I won't be party to making it worse."

"In other words," Blades replied, "you'd rather be party to sabotage. I'm proposing an act of legitimate self-defense."

"*If* there actually is a conspiracy to destroy the Station."

"Adam, you're a spaceman. You know how the Navy operates. Can you swallow that story about a missile getting loose by accident?"

Janichevski bit his lip. The sounds from outside filled the captain's cabin, voices, footfalls, whirr of machines and clash of doors, as the *Pallas Castle* readied for departure. Blades waited.

"You may be right," said Janichevski at length, wretchedly. "Though why Hulse should jeopardize his career—"

"He's not. There's a scapegoat groomed back home, you can be sure. Like some company that'll be debarred from military contracts for a while . . . and get nice fat orders in other fields. I've kicked around the System enough to know how that works."

"If you're wrong, though . . . if this is an honest blunder . . . then you risk committing treason."

"Yeah. I'll take the chance."

"Not I. No. I've got a family to support," Janichevski said.

Blades regarded him bleakly. "If the Essjays get away with this stunt, what kind of life will your family be leading, ten years from now? It's not simply that we'll be high-class peons in the Belt. But tied hand and foot to a shortsighted government, how much progress will we be able to make? Other countries have colonies out here too, remember, and some of them are already giving their people a freer hand than we've got. Do you want the Asians, or the Russians, or even the Europeans, to take over the asteroids?"

"I can't make policy."

"In other words, mama knows best. Believe, obey, anything put out by some bureaucrat who never set foot beyond Luna. Is that your idea of citizenship?"

"You're putting a mighty fine gloss on bailing yourself out!" Janichevski flared.

"Sure, I'm no idealist. But neither am I a slave," Blades hesitated. "We've been friends too long, Adam, for me to try bribing you. But if worst comes to worst, we'll cover for you . . . somehow . . . and if contrariwise we win, then we'll soon be hiring captains for our own ships and you'll get the best offer any spaceman ever got."

"No. Scram. I've work to do."

Blades braced himself. "I didn't want to say this. But I've already informed a number of my men. They're as mad as I am. They're waiting in the terminal. A monkey wrench or a laser torch makes a pretty fair weapon. We can take over by force. That'll leave you legally in the clear. But with so many witnesses around, you'll have to prefer charges against us later on."

Janichevski began to sweat.

"We'll be sent up," said Blades. "But it will still have been worth it."

"Is it really that important to you?"

"Yes. I admit I'm no crusader. But this is a matter of principle."

Janichevski stared at the big red-haired man for a long while. Suddenly he stiffened. "O.K. On that account, and no other, I'll go along with you."

Blades wobbled on his feet, near collapse with relief. "Good man!" he croaked.

"But I will not have any of my officers or crew involved."

Blades rallied and answered briskly, "You needn't. Just issue orders that my boys are to have access to the scoopships. They can install the equipment, jockey the boats over to the full balloons, and even couple them on."

Janichevski's fears had vanished once he made his decision, but now a certain doubt registered. "That's a pretty skilled job."

"These are pretty skilled men. It isn't much of a maneuver, not like making a Jovian sky dive."

"Well, O.K., I'll take your word for their ability. But suppose the *Altair* spots those boats moving around?"

"She's already several hundred kilometers off, and getting farther away, running a search curve which I'm betting my liberty—and my honor; I certainly don't want to hurt my own country's Navy—I'm betting that search curve is guaranteed not to find the missile in time. They'll spot the *Pallas* as you depart—oh, yes, our people will be aboard as per orders—but no finer detail will show in so casual an observation."

"Again, I'll take your word. What else can I do to help?"

"Nothing you weren't doing before. Leave the piratics to us. I'd better get back." Blades extended his hand. "I haven't got the words to thank you, Adam."

Janichevski accepted the shake. "No reason for thanks. You dragooned me." A grin crossed his face. "I must confess though, I'm not sorry you did."

*

Blades left. He found his gang in the terminal, two dozen engineers and rockjacks clumped tautly together.

"What's the word?" Carlos Odonaju shouted.

"Clear track," Blades said. "Go right aboard."

"Good. Fine. I always wanted to do something vicious and destructive," Odonaju laughed.

"The idea is to prevent destruction," Blades reminded him, and proceeded toward the office.

Avis met him in Corridor Four. Her freckled countenance was distorted by a scowl. "Hey, Mike, wait a minute," she said, low and hurriedly. "Have you seen La Ziska?"

"The leftenant? Why, no. I left her with you, remember, hoping you could calm her down."

"Uh-huh. She was incandescent mad. Called us a pack of bandits and—But then she started crying. Seemed to break down completely. I took her to your cabin and went back to help Jimmy. Only, when I checked there a minute ago, she was gone."

"What? Where?"

"How should I know? But that she-devil's capable of anything to wreck our chances."

"You're not being fair to her. She's got an oath to keep."

"All right," said Avis sweetly. "Far be it from me to prevent her fulfilling her obligations. Afterward she may even write you an occasional letter. I'm sure that'll brighten your Rehab cell no end."

"What can she do?" Blades argued, with an uneasy sense of whistling in the dark. "She can't get off the asteroid without a scooter, and I've already got Sam's gang working on all the scooters."

"Is there no other possibility? The radio shack?"

"With a man on duty there. That's out." Blades patted the girl's arm.

"O.K., I'll get back to work. But . . . I'll be so glad when this is over, Mike!"

Looking into the desperate brown eyes, Blades felt a sudden impulse to kiss their owner. But no, there was too much else to do. Later, perhaps. He cocked a thumb upward. "Carry on."

Too bad about Ellen, he thought as he continued toward his office. *What an awful waste, to make a permanent enemy of someone with her kind of looks. And personality—Come off that stick, you clabberhead! She's probably the marryin' type anyway.*

INDUSTRIAL REVOLUTION

In her shoes, though, what would I do? Not much; they'd pinch my feet. But—damnation, Avis is right. She's not safe to have running around loose. The radio shack? Sparks is not one of the few who've been told the whole story and co-opted into the plan. She could—

Blades cursed, whirled, and ran.

His way was clear. Most of the men were still in their dorms, preparing to leave. He traveled in huge low-gravity leaps.

The radio shack rose out of the surface near the verandah. Blades tried the door. It didn't budge. A chill went through him. He backed across the corridor and charged. The door was only plastiboard—

He hit with a thud and a grunt, and rebounded with a numbed shoulder. But it looked so easy for the cops on 3V!

No time to figure out the delicate art of forcible entry. He hurled himself against the panel, again and again, heedless of the pain that struck in flesh and bone. When the door finally, splinteringly gave way, he stumbled clear across the room beyond, fetched up against an instrument console, recovered his balance, and gaped.

The operator lay on the floor, swearing in a steady monotone. He had been efficiently bound with his own blouse and trousers, which revealed his predilection for maroon shorts with zebra stripes. There was a lump on the back of his head, and a hammer lay close by. Ellen must have stolen the tool and come in here with the thing behind her back. The operator would have had no reason to suspect her.

She had not left the sender's chair, not even while the door was under attack. Only a carrier beam connected the Sword with the *Altair*. She continued doggedly to fumble with dials and switches, trying to modulate it and raise the ship.

"Praises be . . . you haven't had advanced training . . . in radio," Blades choked. "That's . . . a long-range set . . . pretty special system—" He weaved toward her. "Come along, now."

She spat an unladylike refusal.

Theoretically, Blades should have enjoyed the tussle that followed. But he was in poor shape at the outset. And he was a good deal worse off by the time he got her pinioned.

"O.K.," he wheezed. "Will you come quietly?"

She didn't deign to answer, unless you counted her butting him in the nose. He had to yell for help to frog-march her aboard ship.

*

"*Pallas Castle* calling NASS *Altair*. Come in, *Altair*."

The great ovoid swung clear in space, among a million cold stars. The asteroid had dwindled out of sight. A radio beam flickered across emptiness. Within the hull, the crew and a hundred refugees sat jammed together. The air was thick with their breath and sweat and waiting.

Blades and Chung, seated by the transmitter, felt another kind of thickness, the pull of the internal field. Earth-normal weight dragged down every movement; the enclosed cabin began to feel suffocatingly small. *We'd get used to it again pretty quickly*, Blades thought. *Our bodies would, that is. But our own selves, tied down to Earth forever—no.*

The vision screen jumped to life. "NASS *Altair* acknowledging *Pallas Castle*," said the uniformed figure within.

"O.K., Charlie, go outside and don't let anybody else enter," Chung told his own operator.

INDUSTRIAL REVOLUTION

The spaceman gave him a quizzical glance, but obeyed. "I wish to report that evacuation of the Sword is now complete," Chung said formally.

"Very good, sir," the Navy face replied. "I'll inform my superiors."

"Wait, don't break off yet. We have to talk with your captain."

"Sir? I'll switch you over to—"

"None of your damned chains of command," Blades interrupted. "Get me Rear Admiral Hulse direct, toot sweet, or I'll eat out whatever fraction of you he leaves unchewed. This is an emergency. I've got to warn him of an immediate danger only he can deal with."

The other stared, first at Chung's obvious exhaustion, then at the black eye and assorted bruises, scratches, and bites that adorned Blades' visage. "I'll put the message through Channel Red at once, sir." The screen blanked.

"Well, here we go," Chung said. "I wonder how the food in Rehab is these days."

"Want me to do the talking?" Blades asked. Chung wasn't built for times as hectic as the last few hours, and was worn to a nubbin. He himself felt immensely keyed up. He'd always liked a good fight.

"Sure." Chung pulled a crumpled cigarette from his pocket and began to fill the cabin with smoke. "You have a larger stock of rudeness than I."

Presently the screen showed Hulse, rigid at his post on the bridge. "Good day, gentlemen," he said. "What's the trouble?"

"Plenty," Blades answered. "Clear everybody else out of there; let your ship orbit free a while. And seal your circuit."

Hulse reddened. "Who do you think you are?"

"Well, my birth certificate says Michael Joseph Blades. I've got some news for you concerning that top-secret gadget you told us about. You wouldn't want unauthorized personnel listening in."

Hulse leaned forward till he seemed about to fall through the screen. "What's this about a hazard?"

"Fact. The *Altair* is in distinct danger of getting blown to bits."

"Have you gone crazy? Get me the captain of the *Pallas*."

"Very small bits."

Hulse compressed his lips. "All right, I'll listen to you for a short time. You had better make it worth my while."

He spoke orders. Blades scratched his back while he waited for the bridge to be emptied and wondered if there was any chance of a hot shower in the near future.

"Done," said Hulse. "Give me your report."

Blades glanced at the telltale. "You haven't sealed your circuit, admiral."

Hulse said angry words, but complied. "Now will you talk?"

"Sure. This secrecy is for your own protection. You risk court-martial otherwise."

Hulse suppressed a retort.

*

"O.K., here's the word." Blades met the transmitted glare with an almost palpable crash of eyeballs. "We decided, Mr. Chung and I, that any missile rig as haywire as yours represents a menace to navigation and public safety. If you can't control your own nuclear weapons, you shouldn't be at large. Our charter gives us local authority as peace officers. By virtue thereof and so on and so forth, we ordered certain precautionary steps taken. As a result, if that war head goes off, I'm sorry to say that NASS *Altair* will be destroyed."

"Are you . . . have you—" Hulse congealed. In spite of everything, he was a competent officer, Blades decided. "Please explain yourself," he said without tone.

"Sure," Blades obliged. "The Station hasn't got any armament, but trust the human race to juryrig that. We commandeered the scoopships belonging to this vessel and loaded them with Jovian gas at maximum pressure. If your missile detonates, they'll dive on you."

Something like amusement tinged Hulse's shocked expression. "Do you seriously consider that a weapon?"

"I seriously do. Let me explain. The ships are orbiting free right now, scattered through quite a large volume of space. Nobody's aboard them. What is aboard each one, though, is an autopilot taken from a scooter, hooked into the drive controls. Each 'pilot has its sensors locked onto your ship. You can't maneuver fast enough to shake off radar beams and mass detectors. You're the target object, and there's nothing to tell those idiot computers to decelerate as they approach you.

"Of course, no approach is being made yet. A switch has been put in every scooter circuit, and left open. Only the meteorite evasion units are operative right now. That is, if anyone tried to lay alongside one of those scoopships, he'd be detected and the ship would skitter away. Remember, a scoopship hasn't much mass, and she does have engines designed for diving in and out of Jupe's gravitational well. She can out-accelerate either of our vessels, or any boat of yours, and out-dodge any of your missiles. You can't catch her."

Hulse snorted. "What's the significance of this farce?"

"I said the autopilots were switched off at the moment, as far as heading for the target is concerned. But each of those switches is coupled to two other units. One is simply the sensor box. If you withdraw beyond a certain distance, the switches will close. That is, the 'pilots will be turned on if you try to go beyond range of the beams now locked onto you. The other unit we've installed in every boat is an ordinary two-for-a-dollar radiation meter. If a nuclear weapon goes off, anywhere within a couple of thousand kilometers, the switches will also close. In either of those cases, the scoopships will dive on you.

"You might knock out a few with missiles, before they strike. Undoubtedly you can punch holes in them with laser guns. But that won't do any good, except when you're lucky enough to hit a vital part. Nobody's aboard to be killed. Not even much gas will be lost, in so short a time.

"So to summarize, chum, if that rogue missile explodes, your ship will be struck by ten to twenty scoopships, each crammed full of concentrated Jovian air. They'll pierce that thin hull of yours, but since they're already pumped full beyond the margin of safety, the impact will split them open and the gas will whoosh out. Do you know what Jovian air does to substances like magnesium?

"You can probably save your crew, take to the boats and reach a Commission base. But your nice battleship will be *ganz kaput*. Is your game worth that candle?"

"You're totally insane! Releasing such a thing—"

"Oh, not permanently. There's one more switch on each boat, connected to the meteorite evasion unit and controlled by a small battery. When those batteries run down, in about twenty hours, the 'pilots will be turned off completely. Then we can spot the scoopships by radar and pick 'em up. And you'll be free to leave."

"Do you think for one instant that your fantastic claim of acting legally will stand up in court?"

"No, probably not. But it won't have to. Obviously you can't make anybody swallow your yarn if a *second* missile gets loose. And as for the first one, since it's failed in its purpose, your bosses aren't going to want the matter publicized. It'd embarrass them to no end, and serve no purpose except revenge on Jimmy and me—which there's no point in taking, since the Sword would still be privately owned. You check with Earth, admiral, before shooting off your mouth. They'll tell you that both parties to this quarrel had better forget about legal action. Both would lose.

"So I'm afraid your only choice is to find that missile before it goes off."

"And yours? What are your alternatives?" Hulse had gone gray in the face, but he still spoke stoutly.

Blades grinned at him. "None whatsoever. We've burned our bridges. We can't do anything about those scoopships now, so it's no use trying to scare us or arrest us or whatever else may occur to you. What we've done is establish an automatic deterrent."

"Against an, an attempt . . . at sabotage . . . that only exists in your imagination!"

Blades shrugged. "That argument isn't relevant any longer. I do believe the missile was released deliberately. We wouldn't have done what we did otherwise. But there's no longer any point in making charges and denials. You'd just better retrieve the thing."

Hulse squared his shoulders. "How do I know you're telling the truth?"

"Well, you can send a man to the Station. He'll find the scooters lying gutted. Send another man over here to the *Pallas*. He'll find the scoopships gone. I also took a few photographs of the autopilots being installed and the ships being cast adrift. Go right ahead. However, may I remind you that the fewer people who have an inkling of this little intrigue, the better for all concerned."

Hulse opened his mouth, shut it again, stared from side to side, and finally slumped the barest bit. "Very well," he said, biting off the words syllable by syllable. "I can't risk a ship of the line. Of course, since the rogue is still farther away than your deterrent allows the *Altair* to go, we shall have to wait in space a while."

"I don't mind."

"I shall report the full story to my superiors at home . . . but unofficially."

"Good. I'd like them to know that we asterites have teeth."

"Signing off, then."

Chung stirred. "Wait a bit," he said. "We have one of your people aboard, Lieutenant Ziska. Can you send a gig for her?"

"She didn't collaborate with us," Blades added. "You can see the evidence of her loyalty, all over my mug."

"Good girl!" Hulse exclaimed savagely. "Yes, I'll send a boat. Signing off."

*

61

INDUSTRIAL REVOLUTION

The screen blanked. Chung and Blades let out a long, ragged breath. They sat a while trembling before Chung muttered, "That skunk as good as admitted everything."

"Sure," said Blades, "But we won't have any more trouble from him."

Chung stubbed out his cigarette. Poise was returning to both men. "There could be other attempts, though, in the next few years." He scowled. "I think we should arm the Station. A couple of laser guns, if nothing else. We can say it's for protection in case of war. But it'll make our own government handle us more carefully, too."

"Well, you can approach the Commission about it." Blades yawned and stretched, trying to loosen his muscles. "Better get a lot of other owners and supervisors to sign your petition, though." The next order of business came to his mind. He rose. "Why don't you go tell Adam the good news?"

"Where are you bound?"

"To let Ellen know the fight is over."

"Is it, as far as she's concerned?"

"That's what I'm about to find out. Hope I won't need an armored escort." Blades went from the cubicle, past the watchful radioman, and down the deserted passageway beyond.

The cabin given her lay at the end, locked from outside. The key hung magnetically on the bulkhead. Blades unlocked the door and tapped it with his knuckles.

"Who's there?" she called.

"Me," he said. "May I come in?"

"If you must," she said freezingly.

He opened the door and stepped through. The overhead light shimmered off her hair and limned her figure with shadows. His heart bumped. "You, uh, you can come out now," he faltered. "Everything's O.K."

She said nothing, only regarded him from glacier-blue eyes.

"No harm's been done, except to me and Sparks, and we're not mad," he groped. "Shall we forget the whole episode?"

"If you wish."

"Ellen," he pleaded, "I had to do what seemed right to me."

"So did I."

He couldn't find any more words.

"I assume that I'll be returned to my own ship," she said. He nodded. "Then, if you will excuse me, I had best make myself as presentable as I can. Good day, Mr. Blades."

"What's good about it?" he snarled, and slammed the door on his way out.

Avis stood outside the jampacked saloon. She saw him coming and ran to meet him. He made swab-O with his fingers and joy blazed from her. "Mike," she cried, "I'm so happy!"

The only gentlemanly thing to do was hug her. His spirits lifted a bit as he did. She made a nice armful. Not bad looking, either.

*

"Well," said Amspaugh. "So that's the inside story. How very interesting. I never heard it before."

"No, obviously it never got into any official record," Missy said. "The only announcement made was that there'd been a near accident, that the Station tried to make counter-missiles out of scoopships, but that the quick action of NASS *Altair* was what saved the situation. Her captain was commended. I don't believe he ever got a further promotion, though."

"Why didn't you publicize the facts afterwards?" Lindgren wondered. "When the revolution began, that is. It would've made good propaganda."

"Nonsense," Missy said. "Too much else had happened since then. Besides, neither Mike nor Jimmy nor I wanted to do any cheap emotion-fanning. We knew the asterites weren't any little pink-bottomed angels, nor the people back sunward a crew of devils. There were rights and wrongs on both sides. We did what we could in the war, and hated every minute of it, and when it was over we broke out two cases of champagne and invited as many Earthsiders as we could get to the party. They had a lot of love to carry home for us."

A stillness fell. She took a long swallow from her glass and sat looking out at the stars.

"Yes," Lindgren said finally, "I guess that was the worst, fighting against our own kin."

"Well, I was better off in that respect than some," Missy conceded. "I'd made my commitment so long before the trouble that my ties were nearly all out here. Twenty years is time enough to grow new roots."

"Really?" Orloff was surprised. "I haven't met you often before, Mrs. Blades, so evidently I've had a false impression. I thought you were a more recent immigrant than that."

"Shucks, no," she laughed. "I only needed six months after the *Altair* incident to think things out, resign my commission and catch the next Belt-bound ship. You don't think I'd have let a man like Mike get away, do you?"